THE MYSTERIES OF STAR GROVE: HEAT

(THE MYSTERIES OF STAR GROVE, #1)

JESSICA SORENSEN

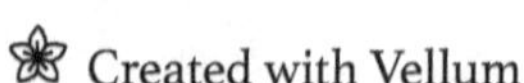 Created with Vellum

CONFUSED IS MY MIDDLE
NAME LATELY

ELLA

Sometimes I feel as if the ground is about to open up and swallow me whole. And sometimes, on mornings like now, I kind of wish it would. I'd way rather be stuck in some dark, bottomless abyss than have to deal with the shit that is my life right now.

"You're going to have to find a way to bail me out," my dad says to me through the phone.

It's five o'clock in the morning—on a school day, I might add—and he's calling me from jail. He hasn't told me why he was arrested, but I have a pretty good guess—something alcohol-related.

"I can't come bail you out right now." I rub the sleepiness from my eyes then glance at the window. Awesome. The damn sun isn't even up yet. "I have to get ready for school in, like, an hour."

"Yeah, so?" he slurs into the phone. "An hour's enough time to come get me."

Awesome. He's still drunk. Then again, when isn't he?

"No, it's not. And we don't have enough extra cash for bail money." I scoot to the edge of my bed and lower my feet onto the floor. "You're just going to have to wait it out ... How long are you supposed to be in there for?"

"Ella ..." The slur still remains in his voice, but his tone is now laced with irrita-tion. "I'm not going to wait. You're going to come bail me out now ... I have to be some-where today ... A work thing."

I roll my eyes. He's so full of shit. My dad hasn't had a job for a couple of weeks, since he got fired for showing up to his last job drunk. It's basically the same reason he was fired from his previous five jobs. More than likely, the real reason he wants to be out of jail so badly is he probably needs another drink. It's all he really does anymore—go to the bar and drink. He's been this way for as long as I can remember, but it has gotten worse lately. Honestly, I'm not even sure where he gets the money to buy drinks since we're broke. I would know since I take care of the finances. I have since I was twelve and realized my mother was too ill to do it herself, my older brother Dean was too irresponsible, and my dad ... well, I think this phone call explains everything.

"You don't have a job right now." I stand up and stretch my arms above my head. "And, like I said, I don't have the time to bail you out, nor do we have the money. And I don't even have my learner's permit, so I'd have to walk down to the station, and it's freezing outside."

I know for a fact it is since 1). It's always cold in Star Grove from September to May, and right now it's November. And 2). There's a layer of frost on my bedroom window.

"I thought you got your license already," my dad murmurs. "You're sixteen. Why haven't you?"

"I'm barely fifteen." I'd be hurt, except he's drunk and probably isn't much aware of anything he's saying. Plus, this isn't the first time he's forgotten how old I am. "I can't get my permit for another few months."

"You've driven before."

"Yeah, but that was an emergency." *When I had to drive Mom to the hospital.*

It happened about six months ago. She was having an episode and wouldn't calm down. Dean and my dad weren't home, and I couldn't get ahold of my best friend Micha, who lives next door to me. He has his learner's permit and would've driven me in a heartbeat, but I couldn't get him to answer his phone that night, which was a bit strange—he almost always answers my calls. In fact, we're usually attached at the hip. But that night he'd gone out of town with his mom and his phone was out of service. And while I have a couple of other friends, I'm not close enough with them to feel comfortable enough to call them up and ask them for a ride to the hospital, especially with the condition my mom was in at the time.

My mom was diagnosed with a bipolar disorder, and sometimes she has grandiose delusions. During them, she talks a lot about these crazy things she believes she can do. For example, she once thought she could fly.

Micha has seen her like this and so has his mom, but no one else outside of my family has. Truthfully, I'm not even sure Dean has since he's rarely around. He graduates at the end of this year and all he talks about is how he's going to take off the day he's given his diploma. I secretly envy him for being able to say that, for not caring about anyone else. Sometimes I wish I could just say to hell with taking care of my drunk dad and ill mother and live my life without worry. But then, who would be here to take my mom to the hospital and make sure she doesn't actually try to fly? Who would pay the bills? Who would pick my dad's sorry ass up from the bar when the bartender threatens to call the police if no one picks him up?

"Look, Ella, just come get me, okay?" my dad says in somewhat of a panic. "Have Micha drive you or have his mom. Just find a damn way to get me out of here, because there's no way in hell I'm staying here until tomorrow ... I can't." His voice cracks.

I'd feel bad for him, except I know the reason he wants to be bailed out.

He wants to drink.

"Why are you even in there anyway?" I ask.

He doesn't answer right away and I start to wonder if he fell asleep.

"I can't remember," he finally says.

More than likely because he was too drunk.

He's always drunk

"You're only going to be in there for twenty-four hours," I say. "I don't need to come bail you out."

"Ella, goddammit," he says, growing more irritated.

I hang up on him.

Yeah, it might be a jerk move to leave my dad in jail, but I've learned over the years that bailing him out really doesn't do him any good. And besides, at least during the twenty-four hours he's behind bars, he can sober up. Although, that'll only last until he's released.

I probably sound like a huge pessimist

right now, but there's a certain point where someone's done the same thing so many times that you stop believing they're going to change. Plus, my dad never makes any promises to change, so ...

"Ella, are you awake?" my mom calls out from her room.

Worry creeps through me as I make my way out of the room and down the hallway, because it's a little weird she's up this early.

It's beyond freezing, making goosebumps sprout across my arms. I can't turn the heat up, though—can't afford it—so all I can do is dress in layers. Right now, I'm sporting an old pair of flannel pajama bottoms I stole from Micha, along with a hoodie that's also his.

I've always borrowed his clothes and, back in the day, they used to fit me. But when we turned fourteen or so, he hit a growth spurt and now is a handful of inches taller than my five-foot-nine frame. He's also gotten a bit more muscular, so his clothes are a bit too big for me. I still wear them, though. At least his pajamas. And while I'll never, ever admit this to anyone aloud, part of the reason I do it is because his clothes smell like him, and I find his scent comforting. But Micha *is* my comfort in my crazy life, so—

"Ella!" my mom shouts, her voice now laced with panic. "Where are you?"

"I'm right here." I push open her bedroom door and find her sitting up in bed, clutching something in her hand. She looks exhausted. Dark circles reside under her eyes, and her hair is a mess of tangles, making me wonder if she slept at all last night or if she just lied awake in bed, like she sometimes does. "What's wrong?"

"I just got a call from your father. He's been arrested and needs our help." She extends her hand toward me. "Take this money and go bail him out." She unfolds her fingers, revealing a wad of cash.

I frown. "Dad called you?"

She nods, urging me to take the money. "And he needs our help now, so go. Help him."

I eyeball the money dubiously. "Where'd you get the cash, Mom?"

She shrugs. "I've been saving up."

Yeah, I'm not buying into that, but at the same time, getting her to tell the truth can be nearly impossible. For instance, the fact that there's a Porsche parked in the crappy garage of our rundown house that's in the middle of a low-income neighborhood. The title to the car has my mom's name on it, yet no one really knows how the hell she got it. She also refuses to sell it, no matter how many times I've thrown the idea out there. Part of me worries she stole it, and I've secretly been waiting for the cops to show up and arrest her, but it hasn't happened yet. Still doesn't mean I don't believe it won't.

"Mom." I choose my next words carefully; knowing that rationalizing with her can be complicated. "I know Dad told you he needs help, but trust me, he really doesn't. He's only going to be in jail for twenty-four hours and for something I'm sure he did ... And it might be good for him to stay there. It'll give him some time to sober up. And we should save our money for stuff like bills."

Shaking her head, she grabs my hand and puts the cash into my palm. "We can't just let him rot in jail. We need to save him, Ella. So, take this money and go save your father." Her eyes are wild and filled with worry.

Pressing my lips together, I wrap my fingers around the cash and nod. "Okay."

She visibly relaxes. "Thanks, sweetie." She rests back in her bed. "You're a good kid, you know that?"

I force a smile. While I like when she's nice to me, I know her upbeat mood is fleeting. And when it nosedives ... well, things get dark really fast.

"Have you taken your meds this morning yet?" I ask. When she shakes her head, I back toward the door. "I'll go get them for you, okay?"

She nods then lies down. "Thanks. I don't know what I'd do without you."

I've thought that a lot, too, which is why, deep down, I know I'll never get to leave Star Grove, even though Micha and I made a pact that one day we would leave together. It'll never happen for me. Not when I have a drunk for a father and a mom who needs taken care of all the time.

Forcing another smile, I leave her room and go down to the kitchen to get her medication. The counters are littered with beer bottles and dishes that need to be cleaned, the garbage needs to be taken out, and I'm not even sure how long it's been since the floor was mopped. I've been slacking off on my chores lately, so I make a mental note to clean the house today when I get home from school, even though Micha will probably want me to hang out with him. I'll have to tell him no, even though I do hate telling him that. And I really hate not being able to go out. It's the only time I get to feel like a normal fifteen-year-old. Well, normal might be a stretch. I'm not sure if I've ever really felt normal.

Sighing at the thought, I grab my mom's medicine bottle from the cupboard, shake a pill out, and then fill up a glass of water before heading back upstairs. When I enter her room, she's already fallen asleep and is pretty out of it when I wake her up to take her pill. The second she takes it, she goes right back to sleep, something I'm grateful for because it means that she'll hopefully stay out of trouble while I'm at school.

After I leave the room, I wander back to my room to stash the cash she gave me, because I'm not going to use it to bail my dad out of jail. Then I grab a pair of black jeans, a grey shirt, and some clean underwear and a bra from my dresser before heading to the bathroom to take a shower.

It's not a surprise when I can't get the water to heat up—probably because the water heater broke again—so I end up taking an ice-cold one. By the time I climb out, my lips are tinted blue and my fingers are numb.

Shivering and chattering, I pull on my clothes then comb my fiery-red hair, something I inherited from my mother, although hers is more auburn than red and way prettier, in my opinion.

I'm not much of a makeup girl, but I have been dabbing on some kohl eyeliner and lip gloss lately. I doubt I'll ever be one of those girls who covers her face with makeup. It just seems too time-consuming, and I already don't have a lot of extra time as it is. Plus, I really don't get the point of caking stuff on all over my face just to wash it off at night. Besides, makeup is super expensive.

Once I'm all done getting ready, I return to my bedroom. It's still early enough that I don't need to leave for school, so I plan on getting out my sketchbook and spending some time working on my mid-term project for art class, but when I enter my room, I realize my plans have gone out the window. Literally, since the window is open.

"Dude, what're you doing?" I ask Micha as he ducks through my bedroom window. "It's freezing outside."

His black boots hit the floor with a thud. "Yeah, so? Like that's ever stopped me before."

True, but still.

I move to close the window while he rakes his fingers through his blond locks that hang into his aqua eyes. Snow dots his black jeans and matching hoodie, which means ...

I glance outside as I pull the window shut then grimace. "Shit, it's snowing."

"Isn't it always snowing?" he remarks, flopping down onto my bed.

"It wasn't when I woke up, and I was kind of hoping it'd stay that way." I sigh, turning away from the window.

"Well, that was very optimistic of you," he teases with a grin.

"I know, right?" I sink down onto the edge of the bed beside his feet. "It's very out of character for me."

His smile fades a bit. "What's wrong?"

I shrug. "Nothing."

"Liar." He sits up and scoots over beside me. "You know I can read you, right? Which means I know when you're lying, sad, pissed off—I know everything about you, Ella May."

His statement is pretty true, but not entirely. There are a couple of things Micha doesn't know about me, and I want to keep it that way. Not that I don't trust him with my secrets—I've known him since I was, like, four years old, and he's done nothing but show his trustworthiness. I just worry he might not like me as much if he knew some of the thoughts I had, how I sometimes wish I could just take off without telling anyone and never come back. Although, I think I'd probably end up telling him because I'd miss him too much.

He gives me a funny look. "You look like you're doubting my mad know-everything-about-you skills."

"No one knows everything about someone," I point out, wishing he couldn't read me so well. "I mean, I know a lot of stuff about you, but I'm sure you have secrets."

I swear, for a flash of a second, worry flickers in his eyes. But then a smile pulls at his lips.

"We should play a game of Truth or Dare so we can find out each other's secrets," he says, seeming pretty pleased with himself.

"If we play Truth or Dare, I'm always going to pick dare." I throw him a haughty smirk. "You should know that if you know everything about me."

A wicked grin touches his lips as he lightly pinches my side. I let out the stupidest girly squeal but don't take off running like some girls would. No, I pinch him back, right on the chest.

He curses, leaning back from me. "Why do you always go for my nipple?" he whines as he rubs the spot I just pinched. "I'm starting to think you are obsessed with them. Is that it? Do you have an obsession with my nipples? Because, if so, maybe I should just show them to you. It might help you get over it." He reaches for the hem of his shirt, a grin forming on his lips.

Here's the thing about having a guy for a best friend: I've gotten used to dirty remarks. And I've learned over the years that, if I blush, it's only going to encourage him more.

"Why would seeing your nipples help me get over my obsession?" I question. "Are they like super hairy and gross, and I'm going to take one look at them and be so grossed out that my obsession ends?"

He gives me an unimpressed look. "My nipples are in no way, shape, or form hairy or gross."

I bite back a smirk. "You're the one that said seeing them would end my obsession. I was just wondering why."

He moves his fingers away from the hem of his shirt with a frown on his face. But that frown quickly dissipates and morphs into a grin. "You know what? I'm not going to take what you said personally, since I know for a fact you don't think my nipples are gross."

I arch a brow, pretending to be the epitome of cool, but deep down, his smirk is making me uneasy. "There's no way you can know that since I don't think that."

He sinks his teeth into his bottom lip, appearing pretty damn amused with himself. "Is that why Ethan caught you staring at me shirtless the other day? And according to him, you stared for at least a minute."

I mentally start chewing my own ass out.

Do not blush, Ella. Don't you effing dare. You're only going to make things worse.

The problem is that I was kinda, sorta checking him out the other day while we were at Ethan's parents' shop and were working on Ethan's truck. It was hot inside, at least according to Micha, so he stripped off his shirt. It wasn't anything I hadn't seen before, but it had been a while since I'd last seem him shirtless. It was when I realized he'd gotten a bit more muscular. Not that he has bulging muscles or anything; he's just leaner and toner than he used to be. And yeah, I may have stared a bit, but only because I was a bit shocked by how different he looked. I didn't realize Ethan had noticed me gawking. If I had, I never would've let my eyes linger, because if anyone's going to rat me out, it's going to be Ethan.

I've known him for almost as long as I've known Micha, but we've never gotten along very well. Not that we hate each other. No, we're more like friends who like to torment each other whenever we get a chance. I think it's because our personalities are kind of similar. That's a theory I keep to myself.

"I wasn't staring," I attempt to lie, but I should know better. Micha may not know every single thing about me, but he can read me super well.

He tugs on a strand of my hair. "You're really cute when you lie."

I lean back to where he can't reach my hair. "Cute when I lie? Seriously, who's the liar?"

"I may be a lot of things, but I'm not a liar. You, on the other hand ..." He smirks.

I pinch his damn nipple again, harder this time.

He laughs, leaning back and rubbing his chest. "You're also cute when you're ruthless."

I shake my head. "I'm not cute, so stop saying that." I stand up, but since it's still early, I don't really have anywhere to go, so it's mainly to just be dramatic. "And you know what? I *was* staring at your chest the other day, but only because I was so shocked how hairy and gross and scrawny it is."

Laughter tickles his throat as he shakes his head. "Now I know that's a lie."

"So you try to tell yourself."

He narrows his eyes, but it's a playful move. "Actually, I've been told many times that I have a very nice chest."

"By who? Blind girls?"

Shaking his head, he lunges at me. He moves so quickly that I have zero time to react, and he manages to get ahold of my waist.

"Hey," I gripe, moving to step back, but he jerks me forward and pushes me onto the bed.

As I land on the mattress, on my back, he moves to climb over me. I know him well enough to know what he's trying to do —pin me down and hold me there until I admit he has a nice chest. I'm not going to go down without a fight, though. I never do.

Before he can get completely on top of me, I shift my legs underneath me then kneel up. He pauses, kneeling in front of me, a smile playing on his lips.

"So, you're going to try to win, huh?" His voice carries a taunt. I know he's totally doing it on purpose, trying to get me all riled up.

I put my hands on my hips. "Do I need to remind you how many of these matches I've won?"

"Yeah, but you haven't won one in a couple of years."

It's beyond annoying that he's right.

"And you want to know why?" he continues, taunting me. "Because I got myself a manly, hairless chest."

I snort a laugh. "Keep telling yourself that, dude."

He narrows his eyes again. "You know what? After I win this one—which I totally will—your punishment's going to be kissing this manly, hairless chest."

While I have zero desire to kiss his chest—at least, that's what I tell myself—

I'm not about to back down from a challenge. It's not my style.

"Fine. But when I win, you have to give
me some driving lessons," I quip.

"Deal," he says way too quickly, which
more than likely means he doesn't care if
he has to give me driving lessons.

"I thought you hated letting me drive," I
say. "That I scare the shit out of you."

He dismisses me with a wave of his
hand then starts rolling up the sleeves of
his jacket. "You only scared me that one
time you nearly ran into that mailbox, but
that doesn't mean I don't like giving you
lessons."

"Liar."

"I'm totally being serious. I mean, think
about it." He starts counting down on his
fingers. "First of all, it gives me time to hang
out with you, which is my favorite thing
ever." He grins as I roll my eyes for at least
the third time in the last minute. "And
second, I know you like driving, and I like
giving you things you like."

His words make me feel stupidly warm
inside, and that warmth makes me very
uncomfortable. Not that he hasn't said stuff

like this to me before; I've just never been good at hearing them. I mean, people wanting to make me happy ... wanting to do stuff for me ... liking me ... it's something I have a hard time understanding.

Of course, while I'm distracted by these confusingly warm feelings swirling around inside me, Micha lunges at me. Thankfully, I manage to jump to my feet and leap out of the way, but he snags the back of my shirt and pulls me back toward him. I reach around to put him in a headlock, but he ducks out of the way and pulls on the back of my shirt, causing me to fall down on the bed. I land on my back with a bounce and hurry to stand up, but he climbs on top of me before I get a chance, putting a knee on each side of me and pinning my arms down beside my head.

"No fair," I gripe, trying to wiggle out from underneath him.

"How is this not fair?" he questions with a shit-eating grin.

"Because you ..." I try to think of a good reason, but I can't, so I let out a frustrated growl instead, to which he responds with a snicker.

"Now that's cute," he teases, holding me down.

I glare at him, but I'm not pissed off at him. No, I'm mad at myself for losing.

I hate losing.

"No, it's not," I growl out.

"Yeah, it is." He leans closer, his eyes glinting wickedly. "And it was a totally fair fight, despite what you think."

"That's not true," I insist.

He arches a brow. "And why not?"

"Because."

"Because why?"

I give him a dirty look. I know what he wants me to say. That it's not fair because he's stronger than me and I know he's stronger because I saw his chest the other day and his muscles. I'm not going to say that, though, because I'm stubborn. So instead, I continue wiggling around until I manage to get my legs hitched around his waist. I smirk at him as I cross my ankles behind his back.

"Ha! Now it's a tie."

He's beyond amused. "How do you figure?"

"Because I have you pinned, too."

"No, you have yourself latched on to me, which is completely different. And I could get away if I wanted to."

I strengthen my hold on him. "If that's true, then prove it."

He raises a brow. "Are you doubting my mad skills?"

I smile sweetly at him then shrug, an awkward move since he still has my arms pinned beside my head.

Wisps of blond hair fall across his forehead as he shakes his head. "Is that a challenge?"

"Isn't this whole thing a challenge?" I quip.

He stares at me for a beat or two longer. "Fine, if that's the way you want to play." Then he pulls my wrists together so he's holding my arms with one hand.

"Hey, what the heck—"

I squeal as he uses his free hand to tickle my thigh.

"Micha! Stop! This is cheating! And I freakin' hate being tickled."

"How the hell is it cheating?" he asks, continuing to tickle me. "It's not my fault I know everything about you, including every one of your tickle spots."

"Yeah, but there's a ... no ... tickling ... rule ..." I'm laughing so hard I can barely get the words out. I also have to pee really, really bad, but I'm not about to unhitch my legs from around him and lose this match. Instead, I focus on tightening my hold on him, lifting my hips and pressing against him as I latch on to him tighter ...

Wait ... What is that pressing against my leg?

My eyes widen when I realize exactly what it is.

As panic sets in, I jerk my legs away.

Micha chuckles, pinning me back down to the bed. "I win," he declares with a grin. Then his grin fizzles as he notes my expression. "What's wrong?"

"Nothing," I lie and not very well.

His brows furrow. "No, something definitely is."

Yeah, there's no way I'm about to tell him that I just felt his man part pressed against my leg.

"I'm just pissed off I lost," I mumble, hoping to hell my cheeks aren't bright red.

His confusion deepens, but then a grin rises on his lips. "You owe my chest a kiss."

"Can I do it a little bit later?" I ask. There's no way I'm going to kiss his chest while he's ...

And why is he even? Because he's turned on? Why the heck would he be turned on while we're wrestling? I know he doesn't see me like *that*, and I sure don't want him to see me like that.

"Sure." He gives me another puzzled look before pushing off me and letting me up.

I don't sit up right away as I work to catch my breath.

As the room grows quiet, this morning's events start to catch up with me again.

That's the thing about Micha. When he's around me and we're goofing around, I sometimes forget about my problems. But the moment a beat of stillness settles between us, it all comes rushing back to me in sharp, potent, consuming waves.

"So, why were you up so early this morning?" he asks, lying down beside me and propping his head up on his elbow.

I turn my head toward him. "How did you know I was up early?"

He absentmindedly plays with my hair. "I was shoveling the driveway so my mom could go to work and saw your light on."

"Oh." I crinkle my nose. "My dad called. He's in jail again and wanted me to bail his sorry ass out."

He frowns. "What's he in for this time?"

I shrug. "Who the hell knows? But since he sounded drunk, my bet is he either got into a bar fight or did something stupid, like piss on someone's front lawn again."

He hesitates. "Are you going to bail him out?"

I shake my head. "He's only going to be in there for twenty-four hours."

He nods. "Might be good to leave him in there then. It'll give him time to sober up."

"That's what I thought, too," I say. "But my mom didn't agree with me. In fact, she gave me a bunch of cash and told me I needed to go bail him out."

A crease forms between his brows. "Where'd she get the cash?"

I huff out a stressed breath. "Who the hell knows? But I'm not about to go spend it on getting my dad out of jail." I wrap my arms around myself as guilt presses against my chest. "Not when the power bill is overdue. Plus, all that's in the fridge is expired milk and a six-pack of beer."

"You're doing the right thing," he tells me, again reading me better than anyone else can. Sometimes he can even read me better than I can read myself.

Still, that doesn't make me feel less guilty for lying to my mom and keeping the money.

"Yeah, I know." Sighing, I sit up and brush strands of my hair out of my face. Then, not wanting to talk about my problems anymore, I change the subject. "So, how are we getting to school today? Is Ethan going to give us a ride, or do we have to take the bus?"

He sits up and stares at me for a moment, probably wanting to ask me more. But, like the good friend he is, he lets the subject drop. "Ethan's picking us up."

I crinkle my nose. "I'm not sure which is worse: the bus or his driving."

"Dude, you're one to talk."

"Hey, I don't even have my learner's

permit yet," I point out. "Give me some time, and I'll be the best driver out of all of us."

His brow curves upward. "Even better than me?"

"For sure."

"Wanna make a wager on that?"

Not really, since I just lost one of our little wagers like two seconds ago. But like I said, I have a really hard time backing down from challenges.

"Yep, you're on." I stick out my hand to make the deal, but he doesn't place his hand in mine.

"How about we make a pact on this one?" A trace of an amused grin tugs at his lips. "If, in six months, you're a better driver than me and Ethan, you get to drive us on a road trip."

"And if I lose?" I ask. "Not that I think I'm going to; I'm curious what you want out of this."

His smile expands. "If you lose, then you have to go on a road trip with us while we drive."

"That's seriously all you want out of this? A road trip?"

He shrugs. "Yeah. And honestly, I don't give a shit who drives."

I eye him over. "So, then what's the point of this pact?"

He shrugs again. "For you to go on a trip with me, something I know you won't do unless it's part of a pact."

True. I have a hard time leaving the house for very long, for several reasons, one being, like take what happened this morning. Had I been here, more than likely my mom would've either talked Dean into using her secret stash of cash to bail our dad out or she would've gone down there herself. Then who the hell knows what would've happened from there?

"I'm not sure I can leave my mom alone for that long."

"We will figure something out ... Maybe my mom can keep an eye on her?"

I waver. While the idea does sound appealing, I'm not sure if it would work. Not to mention we don't have the funds to go on a trip. "Where would we get the money? And where would we go?"

"We'll figure out where we'll go later on," he tells me. "As for where we'll get the money, I'm going to start working at the shop on weekends so I can save up."

"Yeah, but I still need to find a way to come up with some cash."

"I can pay for you."

"No, I don't want you doing that."

"Ella ..." he starts, but I cover his mouth.

"If we're going to do this, I want to pay for myself." I lower my hand from his mouth. "I'll try to find a part-time job."

He looks skeptical but all he says is, "Let me know if you want me to help you find one." Then, shaking out his shoulders, he lifts his hand toward his mouth. "Now to seal the deal."

I scrunch my nose as he spits into his palm. "You know, we really need to find a better way to start making these pacts."

"Nah." He waves me off. "This way is awesome."

"I'm going to have to disagree with you." I spit in my hand anyway and shake his. "Ew, it's all sticky."

He grins deviously. "That's probably because I ate a cinnamon roll right before I came over here."

I pretend to gag. "You're so gross."

"Yeah, so? You're my best friend, so what does that make you?"

"Someone who's tolerant of your gross-ness and who should be rewarded for her patience."

"Oh, you'll be rewarded." Grinning, he stands up. "Tonight, when you get to pucker up and kiss my sexy chest." He makes kissy faces at me.

I pick up a pillow and throw it at him. He ducks out of the way, laughing.

I sigh to myself. *Why, oh why, do I always have to accept a challenge?*

He stops laughing and offers me his hand. "I'll tell you what. If you stop pout-ing, I'll help you clean up your kitchen after school."

"How about you just don't make me kiss your chest?"

He rolls his eyes then snags ahold of my hand. "That's not going to happen."

I let him pull me to my feet. "Why? I'm sure you're just as grossed out by the idea of me kissing your chest as I am."

Instead of answering, he pulls me toward the door, leaving me confused, which kind of seems to be my middle name lately.

By the time we arrive in the kitchen, my confusion has nearly doubled and it's pissing me off that I don't know why. Thankfully someone knocks on the front door, giving me a good distraction.

"I'll be right back," I tell Micha, handing him the broom I was holding.

Then I leave the kitchen and answer the front door.

Standing on the other side is Mrs. Mapleton, the crazy, fifty something year old woman who lives on the corner of our street. And I say crazy because she once chased Micha and I down the sidewalk with a knife. To be fair, we did break her gnomes, but still...

"Hey Mrs. Mapleton." I try not to frown as I greet her, but seriously, why is she here?

She's never been the kind of neighbor to pay a friendly visit.

"Have you seen Harold?" she asks, pushing her glasses higher onto the brim of her nose.

"Harold is your husband, right?" I ask

and she nods. I shake my head. "No, I haven't seen him. Sorry."

"Are you sure?" she questions, narrowing her eyes at me accusingly. "Because the last time I saw him, he was standing outside in the front yard, talking to your mother."

My brows knit. "When was that?"

"Yesterday." Her accusing gaze remains on me.

What she's accusing me of, though, I don't have a clue.

"I'm sorry, Miss Mapleton, but I don't think that was my mom your husband was talking to," I tell her. "She was home all day yesterday." I'd know since I was the one keeping an eye on her.

"Whatever. I know it was her." She backs off the front steps. "Tell your mother that if she's seen *my husband* to let me know, or else I'm going to have to report him missing."

"Um, okay." I close the door, feeling totally lost.

"What was that about?" Micha asks from just behind.

I turn and find him leaning against the

doorframe. "Miss Mapleton was looking for her husband and for some weird reason, she thought my mom would know where he is." I scratch at my arm. "She said she saw my mom talking to him yesterday, but I know my mom was home."

"Mrs. Mapleton's probably just getting confused," Micha remarks. "You know she's a little..." He rotates his finger around his temple. "Remember the gnome incident."

"How can I forget?"

And Micha is probably right. Mrs. Mapleton is probably just getting confused.

Still, I can't shake the feeling that she was implying something by the way she stressed that Harold was *her husband*. Why would she do that, unless...

Unless my mom was having an affair with Harold.

But I know my mom was in our house yesterday, unless she somehow snuck out.

What if she did? What if my mom is having an affair?

"You okay?" Micha asks, pushing away from the doorframe and stepping toward me.

I nod. Then not wanting him to worry, I

put on my best fake smile that I hope he can't see through. "Yeah, I'm fine."

It's the answer I always give when someone asks if I'm okay.

And I've said it so many times that sometimes I can actually almost convince myself it's true.

I'M NOT HOT

Ella

Micha and I spend the next fifteen minutes cleaning the kitchen before someone honks a horn from outside.

"That's probably Ethan," Micha tells me as he sets down the dishrag that he's holding.

I glance at the clock on the microwave. "Why's he here so early?"

"I think he wants to drive up to the cabin."

The cabin is basically a log structure

that resides at the bottom of the mountains that surround Star Grove. The roof is caved in, along with the floor. The entire place looks like it could collapse at any moment, which probably makes it dangerous to be there, which makes it appealing to me.

I don't know why I'm like that, why I crave danger and adrenaline rushes. All I know is that my need for adventure has gotten me in trouble a lot over the years.

I grab my leather jacket off a chair near the back door and put it on. Then I reach to pick my backpack up but pause. "So, he wants to ditch today?"

"Yeah, probably." He tugs on a strand of my hair. "You got a problem with that?"

"Yeah right. I'm glad we're ditching." Especially after the visit from Mrs. Mapleton.

I can't get the idea out of my head that somehow my mom is having an affair.

I need a time out to think about something else.

"Who's ditching?" Dean asks as he wanders into the kitchen.

His messy blue hair needs a dye job; the brown roots showing. He has on a torn T-shirt and pair of worn pajama bottoms, and his eyes are bloodshot, which more than likely means he got stoned last night.

"No one," Micha replies before I get a chance.

Micha has never been a fan of my brother, even though they sometimes play in a band together. Micha plays guitar and sings, and Dean plays the bass and the drums when Ethan doesn't show up. There's also another guy name Jameson, who's Dean's friend. I think he does a bit of everything.

While I love my brother and everything, Dean can be a huge asshole sometimes, so I don't really blame Micha for not liking him. I think the only reason Micha is in the band at all is because he lives and breathes music, and there's not a lot of opportunities in Star Grove.

Micha is definitely the best in the band. He plays the guitar perfectly, his voice is almost otherworldly, and he writes his own music. He's pretty awesome, but I might be biased, being his best friend and all.

Dean cocks a brow at Micha as he opens the fridge. "Yeah, like that sounded convincing ..." He trails off as he glances inside the fridge. "Where the hell is all the food?"

I zip up my jacket. "I haven't had time to go grocery shopping, but I'll try to go tonight." And use part of the money Mom gave me earlier this morning.

"Or you could always go?" Micha says to Dean in a cold tone.

Shaking his head, Dean closes the fridge and turns to face Micha, crossing his arms. "What's your problem lately? First, you get pissed off because I told Ella I didn't want her hanging around while we practice. And now you're getting pissy because why? I don't even know this time."

"I'm pissy because you treat her like shit." Micha nods his head in my direction. "And you act like she's your maid, which she's not."

Dean glares at Micha. "How I treat my sister is none of your damn business."

"She's my best friend, so yeah, it is," Micha snaps, reaching for my hand.

"Guys ..." I start, but they talk over me.

"Best friend, huh?" Dean gives Micha

this insinuating look that I don't quite understand.

Apparently, Micha does, though, and he doesn't like the meaning, because he immediately frowns.

"Yeah, that's what I thought." Looking pretty damn smug, Dean turns around and walks out of the kitchen.

I glance at Micha. "What the hell was that about?"

Gritting his teeth, he shrugs. "I have no idea."

I elevate my brows. "Now who's the liar?"

Micha sighs heavily. "I'm not lying. I just ... don't really want to get into it right now." He seems twitchy, which is so unlike him.

"Okay." I give a short pause as I replay what Dean said that seemed to upset Micha. "Are you not really my best friend? Do you just tell me that, and then, when you're with your guy friends, joke about how I believe you?" I know I sound child-ish, but it's the only reason I can think of as to why Micha reacted the way he did when

Dean seemed to question if I was really Micha's best friend.

Micha gapes at me then suddenly busts up laughing.

Confusion dances inside me. "What the hell's so funny?"

He shakes his head, tears of laughter shining in his eye. "You thinking that we're not really best friends."

I'm still beyond confused and kind of getting annoyed. "And that's funny, why?"

"Because it could never, ever be true." He dramatically presses his free hand to his chest. "You're more than my best friend, Ella May. You're my other half."

Again, a stupid warmth starts to spread throughout my body, but I quickly squash it.

"You're so damn cheesy sometimes. Seriously, if girls heard the crap you said to me, you'd have even more girlfriends than you already do."

He points a finger at me as he pulls me toward the back door. "Hey, I've never had a girlfriend."

I roll my eyes as he yanks open the door and snowflakes trickle in from outside.

"You say that all the time, yet every single weekend, you hook up with someone."

"Yeah, but that doesn't make them my girlfriend."

As we step outside, he draws his hood over his head, while I reach into my pocket to dig out the fingerless gloves that I always keep in there. I slip them on then zip up my jacket, debating whether to go back inside and grab a beanie or not.

"One day, that's going to change." I lift my hand in front of my face as snowflakes land all over me.

He reaches into his pocket and, like a freakin' mind reader, pulls out a beanie. "Nah, that'll never happen." He tugs the beanie over my head then fixes my hair so it's not in my face. "Well, until you finally agree to be my girlfriend."

He's said this to me many times over the last year or so, mostly because he knows it drives me crazy.

I groan, bobbing my head back. "Oh my God, don't start with that crap again, or I'm going to have to kick your ass."

His eyes glint mischievously. "Like you just kicked my ass on your bed earlier?"

I narrow my eyes at him. "That was an unfair match."

"Keep telling yourself that. Deep down, you know I won fairly. And eventually, you're going to have to pay up." He pulls me along with him as he starts down the snow-covered driveway.

Around the neighborhood, people are working on shoveling their driveways, but with how heavy the snow is coming down, it's probably a lost cause. My gaze drifts to Mrs. Mapleton's house, a rundown brick, two-story structure that stands in the middle of a patchy front lawn covered by gnomes.

I try to picture my mom going over there, sneaking in the back door, and...

And what, Ella? You seriously think Mom is somehow sneaking around like that?

Normally, I'd think no way, but when I really think about it, there's been a few times where she's managed to sneak out of the house without me knowing.

"You okay?" Micha asks, drawing my attention back to him.

I try to shove all thoughts of my mom's questionable affair out of my mind and focus on having fun. Or at least pretending to have fun.

"Yeah, I'm okay." I glance at Micha's house. Just on the other side of the fence that divides our properties is the driveway to his house, and it's nearly buried in snow. "But I thought you said you were shoveling the driveway this morning?" I look back to Micha just in time to see him tense. But in a flutter of a snowflake, he relaxes back to his casual self.

"Yeah, but it's snowing so hard it didn't do much good."

I have a feeling he might be lying to me, but about what? I could ask, but then we reach Ethan's truck.

Micha pulls open the driver's side door and gestures for me to get in.

I shake my head. "No way. I'm not sitting bitch again."

"Jesus, do we have to do this every time?" Ethan grumbles from the driver's seat. "Just get in the truck. I've got shit to do this morning." He has a knitted cap pulled over his dark hair, a hooded jacket on, and a cigarette is resting between his fingers, the smoke lacing out through the cracked open window.

"You say that every morning," I remark. When he scowls at me, I smile sweetly at him. "What? You do. And yet, you never actually have anything to do."

"I'm driving your asses around, aren't I?" he quips, ashing his cigarette out the window. "And besides, this morning, I do have stuff to do."

"What?" Micha and I ask simultaneously.

He shrugs, cranking up the heat. "I'm meeting some people up at the cabin."

"Who?" Micha asks, stuffing his hands into his pockets.

"Renee, Jane, Jay, and Steve," he says. "There might be more, but who the hell knows?"

I wrap my arms around myself as the cold starts to seep through my clothes. "So, everyone's ditching today?"

"Yeah," Ethan replies. "It should be a snow day anyway."

"Every day should be a snow day here," I point out then step back and motion for Micha to get into the truck.

He shakes his head. "As much as I love giving you your way, Ethan will have a shit-fit if I try to cuddle up with him while he's driving."

"Just because I'm the chick in our group, doesn't mean I always have to sit bitch," I reply, refusing to budge.

"It's not because you're a chick," Micha insist. "It's because you're the smallest."

"That used to not be true," I grumble, my breath fogging out in front of my face.

"But it is, so ..." He gestures at the truck.

"Well, you're the tallest, so ..." I mimic his gesture.

"Would you two knock it off?" Ethan gripes. When neither of us budges, he adds, "Micha, just put her in the truck so we can go. I'm supposed to pick up Renee in, like, ten minutes."

"Are you two like dating now?" I snicker, knowing my remark is going to piss him off.

He glares at me. "Ha, ha, you're a fucking riot." He gives Micha a pressing look with his brows raised.

I know them well enough to under-stand they're having a silent conversation about me, probably one that has to do with getting me in the truck.

I start to move back when Micha loops his arms around my waist and lifts me up.

"Hey! Not fair," I whine as he hoists me onto the seat. Then he pushes me toward the middle, hurriedly climbs inside, and shuts the door.

I sulk as I get situated in the seat, sitting closer to Micha than Ethan.

"Payback's going to be a bitch," I threaten Micha, but he only smiles.

He grabs Ethan's pack of cigarettes from off the dash, lights up, and cracks the window. Cold air and smoke fills the cab as Ethan backs down the driveway and onto the icy road.

"We need to stop and get breakfast from somewhere," Micha tells Ethan after he takes a drag off his cigarette.

"We will after we pick up Renee," he mumbles, turning down a side street and heading in the direction of Renee's house.

As the snow on the road gets deeper, he shifts his truck into four-wheel drive.

"Why are we even picking her up?" Micha drapes his arm across the back of the seat behind me. "I thought she annoyed the shit out of you."

"Not always," he responds vaguely.

Micha and I trade an amused look then Micha says, "I know Ella just asked this, but now I'm wondering: are you guys dating?"

Ethan blasts him with a dirty look. "You know I don't do relationships. And even if I did, it sure as hell wouldn't be with Renee."

"You seem awfully testy about this." I lean into Micha while smirking at Ethan.

He narrows his eyes. "I'm *not* dating her, so shut the hell up."

"It sure seems like you might be," Micha says, sliding his arm from the back of the seat and putting it around my shoulders.

Ethan's glare deepens, but then a conniving smile tugs at his lips. "Maybe I should be asking you two the same thing. I mean, look at you right now, all cuddled up like a couple."

Instead of getting annoyed, Micha just grins and pulls me closer. "If we were a couple, we'd make a cute one." He presses his cheek against mine.

Ethan pulls a disgusted face and flicks his cigarette out the window.

Shaking my head, I push Micha back. "You're such a weirdo."

"I second that," Ethan says as he parks beside the curb in front of Renee's single-story home. Then he shoves open the door and hops out, muttering, "I'll be right back."

Micha and I watch as he hikes through the snow to the front door.

"Holy crap, did he seriously just go up to the door?" I ask, glancing at Micha.

Micha nods, his eyes glinting with amusement. "I think they might be hooking up."

I crinkle my nose. "Ew."

"Which one are you saying ew to?" he questions with amusement. "Ethan hooking up with Renee or Renee hooking up with Ethan? Or is it just hooking up in general?"

I lift a shoulder, feeling a bit uncomfortable at the mention of hooking up. I mean, it's not like I'm a prude or anything, but the idea of getting that close to anyone ... I don't know, it just makes me feel squirrely inside.

"Maybe all three," I say with another shrug. "But who am I to judge? It's not like I've ever done anything with anyone."

"That's not true."

"Um, yeah, it is."

"No, it's not." He stares at me expectantly, as if waiting for me to figure out what he's referring to. When I don't, he adds, "About a year ago. You and I and the swing set."

"That really doesn't count."

He either pretends to be hurt or is hurt —I'm not quite sure. "How the hell does that not count? We kissed for, like, twenty seconds."

"Because it was a challenge." I start to grow even more squirmy. "We didn't really want to kiss."

"Says who?"

"Says me and you."

"That's not true." He places his hand against his chest. "*I* wanted to kiss you."

I roll my eyes. "Only because you were bored."

"No, I wasn't. I ..." He trails off as Ethan returns to the truck and opens the door.

When he sticks his head in, he looks from me to Micha then at Renee as she opens the passenger door. "Someone's going to have to lap it up."

"Not it!" I call out before anyone else can.

Renee shrugs then moves to climb in. "That's cool with me. I don't mind sitting on Micha's lap."

For the briefest second, a flash of irritation flickers in my chest. But I ignore it, unsure of where it came from.

"Actually, Ella can just sit on mine," Micha says, wrapping his fingers around my waist.

Before I can even react, he lifts me up, slides over, and plants me down onto his lap.

"What the heck is up with you just moving me around whenever you want? I'm not a damn doll," I say as I wiggle around to get situated.

"If you were, though, you'd be a really pretty one," he whispers in my ear.

I whip my head to the side and glare at him. "Watch it with the *P* word, dude."

He lifts up a hand in surrender while resting his other hand on my hip. "My bad. I forgot how much you hate it."

I mentally roll my eyes. He so did not. In fact, I think he secretly calls me pretty because it irks me.

"You two are so cute it's disgusting," Renee mumbles as she hops in beside Micha and shuts the door.

People say stuff like this to Micha and me all the time, like we're this cute couple. It's annoying. Sometimes I quip back with a snarky comeback, but right now, I'm super exhausted from all the crap that happened this morning. And hungry apparently, something my stomach announces as it grumbles loudly.

Micha chuckles, circling his arms around my waist. "Hungry, Ella May?"

I nod, resting back against him. "Yeah, kind of."

He pulls me even closer then tells Ethan, "Stop at the diner so we can feed the gremlin that has apparently taken up residency in Ella's stomach." He brushes his fingers along the bottom of my belly as he says it.

He's done stuff like this before, but lately, these annoying tingles spread across my skin whenever he does, and I have to press my lips together to keep from shivering.

Ethan already has another lit cigarette between his fingers, and ash falls to his lap as he gives Micha a salute. Then he shoves the shifter into drive and steers forward, the truck sliding in the snow.

It takes us about ten minutes to get to the diner when normally it takes about five. The snow is really piling up, enough that a concern starts to rise.

"We might want to go someplace else besides the cabin," Renee says as she stares at the snow flurrying from the sky. "We might not even be able to make it up there."

"And if we do, we might get stuck there," I add.

Honestly, I wouldn't mind getting stuck out in the mountains for a while, but only so I won't have to deal with the drama I know is going to be waiting for me when I get home today.

My mom might be having an affair.

My dad's in jail.

God, life sucks sometimes.

"Yeah, so? That doesn't sound bad to me." Ethan parks at the diner and begins examining the menu in front of us.

The place is straight out of the seventies. The waiters and waitresses skate around outside on roller skates and take orders at vehicles. Well, at least that's how it works in the summer. In the winter, though, they hike through the two feet of snow to do it.

"Of course it doesn't," I reply to Ethan, not bothering to look at the menu. I have a total of two bucks in my pocket, which means I can afford a coffee and a hash brown. "I swear one day you're going to just take off and go live in the mountains."

Ethan bobs his head in agreement, his attention straying to the waitress taking another order.

My gaze wanders to the *help wanted* sign on the diner's door. "Maybe I should work here," I say to no one in particular.

Renee snorts a laugh. "Yeah right."

My gaze slides to her. "What's so funny about that?"

She shrugs, tucking a strand of her short, dark hair behind her ear. "Don't take this the wrong way, but you have zero people skills, and you need that to work at a place where most of your salary relies on tips."

Her words, while irritating, are probably true.

"I don't know about that," Micha disagrees, resting his hand on my leg.

Renee glances at him questioningly. "You think Ella has people skills?"

"No." He grins when I throw a playful dirty look at him. "But she could get a lot of tips if she wanted to."

Renee's brows dip. "How?"

Micha's eyes sparkle as he shrugs. "She's hot, and a lot of times guys will tip a waitress just because she's hot."

Now I give him a real dirty look. "I'm not hot."

He rolls his eyes. "All right, you're not hot."

My jaw ticks and I start to squirm, irritated and confused. I know he's called me pretty a ton of times, but only because he knows it bugs me. But he's never called me hot. No guy has.

Renee's gaze shifts from me to Micha. Then she raises her brows and focuses on the menu, muttering, "You two just need to screw and get it over with."

My fingers curl into fists, and I may have hit her if Micha hadn't brushed his fingers along my thigh.

"Easy, firecracker," he whispers with a hint of laughter in his tone. "Let's try not to get into a fight today. At least until after we eat."

"Fine." I stick my lip out, which causes him to chuckle. "But if she says anything like that again, I'm not going to let it slide." I talk loud enough for her to hear me, but she doesn't reply, pretending to focus on the menu.

Renee knows I can kick her ass if I wanted to. In fact, it wouldn't be the first time I have.

Seconds later, the waitress arrives at our truck. Ethan rolls the window down, letting cold air and snow into the cab.

"What can I get you?" she asks, chattering a bit. Her lips are also kind of blue.

Poor girl. I feel bad she has to be outside in these conditions.

Maybe I don't want to work here. Then again, I can't afford to be picky.

Ethan gives her a flirty grin and starts prattling off his order. I go next, ordering a coffee and a hash brown, and then Micha goes, ordering enough food to feed both him and Ethan. Renee only gets a coffee. Then she lights up a cigarette, rolls down the window, and starts chatting with the guys in the truck parked beside us.

I nearly fall asleep as I wait for our food to arrive, listening to Micha and Ethan talk about the car Micha wants to buy.

I really need to get some good sleep tonight, I think to myself.

Maybe I'll ask Micha to stay over tonight. I sleep better when he's around. Plus, he's like my own personal heater …

"You falling asleep on me there?" Micha whispers in my ear.

My eyelids start to lower…

Then next thing I know I'm waking up.

"Holy crap, did I fall asleep?" I ask, sitting up and rubbing my eyes.

I glance around and realize Micha and I in Ethan's truck, but Ethan and Renee aren't here anymore. And we're parked in front of Jane's house who's a friend of ours.

So I guess everyone decided not to go to the cabin.

Micha nods, his eyes searching mine. "How much sleep did you get last night?"

I shrug. "I don't know. I think I went to bed at like one and woke up at five."

He frowns. "Why'd you go to sleep so late?"

I shrug. "Sometimes I have a hard time falling asleep."

"You don't when I spend the night."

"I know."

"You want me to spend the night tonight?" he asks.

I shrug. I really want him to, but I'm not about to admit it.

He smiles. "All right, I will." Then he shifts me off his lap and slides over to climb out of the truck. Once he gets out, he reaches into the cab, grabs a bag from the dashboard, and a cup of coffee from the cupholder.

"Is that my breakfast?" I ask as I slide to the edge of the seat.

He nods and hands me the goodies. "Yep. You're lucky Ethan didn't eat it. I had to threaten him like ten times."

"He's such a pig," I remark, peering into the bag. "Wait. There's more than just a hash brown in here."

"Because you need to eat more than just a hash brown."

"Micha." I frown, glancing up at him. "We've gone over this. You don't need to take care of me all the time."

"I know I don't need to, but I like to." He signals for me to climb out. "Now come on; let's get inside. I'm freezing my ass off."

I don't budge. "How much do I owe you for the food?"

He gives me a tolerant look. "You know I'm not going to take your money."

"Then I'm going to stick some cash in your pocket when you're not looking," I threaten.

Snowflakes land on the top of his hood

as he shrugs. "Go ahead. I'll just put it right back into your pocket."

I glare at him, but he only laughs and places his hands on my waist.

"Come on. I'll carry you inside."

I close the bag of food. "No thanks. I'd rather use these things I have called legs. They're pretty cool. They can move and carry my body around."

He chuckles, pulling me closer until I'm sitting on the edge of the seat with my legs nestled between his. "I'll carry you so you don't have to get your boots wet." He glances down at my ankle-high, velvet boots. "I have no idea why you wore those today. The snow's going to ruin them."

"I didn't realize I was going to be wading through snow," I point out, hitching my legs around his waist. "I thought we were just going to school, which is usually plowed."

"Well, it's a good thing you have your very own carrying taxi," he teases as I loop my arms around the back of his neck. Then he slips his arms around my waist and steps back from the truck with me holding onto him.

"A taxi who gets me breakfast," I add, clutching on to him.

As I press up against him, I'm reminded of what happened this morning while we were wrestling around. Or, more like what I *felt* ...

"I have a question," I say as he carries me across Jane's front yard.

"What's up?" he asks, shifting my weight in his arms.

I chew on my bottom lip, unsure if I dare ask, but curiosity gets the best of me. "You don't really think I'm hot, right?"

He presses his lips together, his gaze shifting to me. "Do you want the truth or a lie?"

I almost say lie but find myself stupidly saying, "The truth?"

He wavers, his eyes searching mine. "Okay, then yeah, I think you're hot." I'm about to freak out on him, even though it's my own fault that he said it, when he adds, "Don't freak out on me. I'm just stating a fact. And I'm not the only guy who thinks this either."

"Who else thinks this?" I ask, unsure if

I'm annoyed or not that guys are talking about my hotness.

He shrugs. "Guys say it all the time." He pauses as we reach the front door, his eyes searching mine again. "Do you like that they do?"

"No." I'm not sure if that's the truth or not.

His lips sink into a frown, but then he quickly plasters on a smile. "You're such a little liar. You love that guys think you're hot."

"No, I don't." I pinch his chest.

He flinches then grins, his eyes darkening. "You know what? That little pinch just reminded me that you owe my sexy chest a kiss. And I think I'm going to collect when we get inside."

I scowl at him. "Not yet."

"Yep, right now." Then, holding me up with one arm, he pulls the door open and steps inside, leaving me to silently freak out.

FIERY RED LIPSTICK

Ella

I'm trying to calm down as I hang out in the basement with Renee and Jane, but knowing what I'm going to have to do soon is sending panic through me. I try to distract myself the best that I can by devouring the breakfast sandwich, hash brown, and coffee Micha bought me.

"You're being super quiet right now," Renee remarks as I finish off my hash brown.

I shrug, wiping off my hands. "It's not like I'm ever Miss Talkative."

"She has a point." Jane, who's a year older than me and has blonde hair and a lot of piercings, picks up a bottle of vodka that Renee brought over.

Micha, Ethan, and Steve, Jane's boyfriend, wandered off to the garage to check out Steve's new ride. I wanted to go with them, but I was hungry and decided to sit down and eat. Now I'm starting to regret my decision.

"Why don't you talk that much?" Jane asks as she unscrews the cap on the vodka bottle. "Or, well, I should say talk that much to us. You talk to Micha all the time."

I want to say that *I like Micha* but manage to bite my tongue. "Because I think talking is overrated."

Jane nods her head then takes a swig of vodka. "I actually agree with you about that." She passes the bottle to me. "Talking *is* overrated, especially when we can do so much more with our mouths, like drink or make out with a hot guy."

Renee and her laugh while I mentally roll my eyes.

I really should have gone with the guys.

Sighing, I take the bottle and swallow a sip, mostly to calm my freaking nerves over having to kiss Micha's chest. As the thought crosses my mind, I take another swallow then hand the bottle to Renee.

"What was Micha talking about with you before he walked out of here with Ethan and Steve?" Renee asks as she lifts the bottle of vodka toward her mouth. "I heard him say you owed him or something."

I sink back into the worn leather sofa. "Well, to make a long story short, I lost a challenge and now ... I have to kiss his chest."

Renee blinks in surprise. "What the hell was the challenge about?"

I shrug, picking at a loose thread hanging from a hole in my jeans. "Over whether or not he has a hairy, gross chest."

Renee gapes at me. "Please say you were arguing that he doesn't."

"What would be the fun in that?" I question with a smirk.

She shakes her head, still gaping at me.

"Ella, you're seriously the craziest person I've ever met."

"I'll second that," Jane says as she snatches the bottle from Renee. "I mean, Micha's not even my type, but I'll totally admit he's hot. And that includes his chest, because I've seen that guy with his shirt off and ..." She gets a lustful smile on her face. "All I can say is *wow*."

"Wow's an understatement," Renee says, stretching her legs out in front of her. "I saw him a couple of months ago walking around shirtless at the shop and, holy hell, he's gotten hot as hell. One of these days, I'm going to hook up with him." She sneaks a glance in my direction.

"Why're you looking at me like that?" I ask. "If you have something to say, just say it."

The two of them trade a look then Jane sighs and looks at me. "Some of us have been wondering if maybe you and Micha ... If you ..." She hesitates, glancing at Renee.

"Dude, why're you so afraid of her?" Renee asks with an eye roll.

"Um, hello, did you not see her punch Ava last weekend?" Jane sets the bottle down on the cracked coffee table then looks at me. "Seriously, Ella, you're kind of ruthless."

"Ava deserved it," I defend myself. "She tripped Lana for no reason, and she nearly fell into the fire pit."

"Oh, I didn't know that." Jane pauses. "I'm kind of glad you did it then."

"Whatever. We're getting off track," Renee interrupts, twisting to face me. "It's time to confess what's going on with you and Micha, so the rest of us—and by rest of us, I mean me—know whether or not we'll be breaking any rules if we decide to hook up with Micha."

"Aren't you hooking up with Ethan?" I ask, aware I may be deflecting.

Renee gives a half-shrug. "Yeah, so? We're not dating."

"Dude, you two sound just like each other," I say.

"And you're avoiding answering my question," Renee replies. "And I'm starting to think you're doing it on purpose."

I resist a frown, even though my lips really want to pull downward. But if I do, then she'll know the truth. And no one can know the truth—that sometimes it does bother me when Micha hooks up. But it's not because I want him for myself; I just don't want to lose him to anyone else. Which, yes, is selfish, but it's how I feel.

I'm not about to tell anyone that, though.

"If you want to hook up with him, then do it." I shrug, knowing the only reason I'm so chill about saying the words aloud is because I know Micha will never hook up with Renee—she's not his type.

"Who can hook up with who?" Micha asks, appearing in the doorway and making me cringe.

"Um ..." I glance at Renee, who shrugs and looks at Micha.

"A friend of mine wants to hook up with you," she tells him.

Micha's gaze flicks to me then back to her. His brow arches upward. "And why does she need Ella's permission for that?"

Renee shrugs again. "Because sometimes it seems like you two are dating."

A protest works up my throat, but Micha beats me to the punch.

"You know, that remark is kind of

insulting," he says as he makes his way across the room and plops down on the sofa beside me, "since you saw me hook up with Beth last weekend, which would mean I cheated on Ella."

"Oh my God, you did?" I give a mocking gasp, hoping to distract everyone from whether Micha and I are dating.

A smile quirks at his lips as he shucks off his jacket. "I'm sorry, baby. I didn't mean to. Please forgive me."

I cross my arms. "Nope. We're so breaking up. And I want my shirt back."

He tilts his head to the side. "What shirt?"

"That one I got at the concert last month that you stole from me."

"I didn't steal it from you. I bought it for myself."

I fake a pout. "I thought you bought it for me. And now I find out you cheated on me and we're breaking up ... What a shitty morning."

He drums his fingers against his lips. "I'll tell you what. I'll give you the shirt as an apology for cheating on you and making you break up with me. We have to stay friends, though."

"Deal," I agree then grow serious. "Are you really going to give me the shirt?"

He bobs his head up and down. "Yeah, it looks better on you anyway."

And there comes that stupid warmth again.

"Oh my God," Renee groans. "Not dating, my ass. You guys are disgusting. For reals. I'm not even going to bother competing with that."

Micha's brows rise as he glances at me, but I simply shrug, my good mood deflating. I really start questioning why I'm friends with Renee.

"Hey, baby," Steve says to Jane as he enters the room. He's bundled up in a large coat and thick boots, both of which he discards before he plops down onto the sofa. Then he leans in to kiss Jane, and she giggles, kissing him back.

I pull a disgusted face—PDA has never and will never be my thing—and look away only to find Micha observing me curiously.

My brows pull together. "What's that look for?"

He gives a shrug then nudges me over so he can sit down between me and the armrest. "Nothing. I was just thinking."

I rotate toward him and rest my elbow on the back of the sofa. "About what?"

He stretches his arm along the back of the sofa, the crook of his arm resting beside my elbow. "Just life."

"Always such a deep thinker," I tease.

He smiles, but it doesn't quite reach his eyes.

"You want to talk about something?" I ask. "Because it kind of looks like you do."

He glances around at Steve and Jane, who are making out on the sofa, and then at Jane, who's gotten up and is messing around with a dartboard on the wall. Pressing his lips together, he then looks back at me. "I was just thinking about life and being with someone. I mean, in like an actual relationship."

A weird, churning sensation stirs in the pit of my stomach. "Are you saying you want to date someone?" I ask, and he raises a shoulder. The churning sensation gets worse. "Who?"

He stares at me with a puzzled yet

somehow intense look on his face. "I'm not sure yet." He slants back, raking his fingers through his hair. "Honestly, I'm not even sure I could ever date anyone."

The churning sensation lets up a bit but leaves me wondering why. "Why not?"

"I don't know ..." He chews on his bottom lip, his face set in deep thought. "I'd probably suck at being in one since I know shit about them."

My heart aches for him a little bit. "You're talking about your mom?"

When Micha was six, his dad bailed on his family, and he hasn't seen him since. Micha's mom has dated a few times, though, and a couple of those relationships were decent.

He reclines back against the sofa, letting out a loud exhale. "Maybe ... Honestly, I'm not sure what I'm even talking about. I'm just in a weird mood."

I can sense that, but what I can't sense is the exact cause of his weird mood. I want to cheer him up, though, like he always tries to do with me.

"What about your mom and Grady?" I tell him. "Their relationship was pretty good." Which is true. And Micha and I still occasionally visit Grady.

"Yeah, I know." He meets my gaze, staring at me in a way that makes me squirm. Then he suddenly grins. "You know what would cheer me up?"

"Oh God, here we go," I groan, playing along, but part of me is still worried what caused his sullen mood.

Does he really want to be in a relationship? Or was it about something else?

If he does want to date someone, what will that do to our relationship?

"You should be worried." A grin takes over his face as he leans toward me, the scent of cologne, cigarette smoke, and something that only belongs to Micha engulfing my nostrils. "I think it's time for you to pay up."

I shake my head. "Later."

"Nope, it's time." He stands up and reaches for the hem of his shirt.

My heart thunders in my chest, blood roaring in my eardrums. *Is he seriously going to make me do this?*

"I'm not sure what's going on, but keep going," Renee encourages as she puts down the dart she's holding and fixes her attention on Micha.

Grinning, he gradually lifts his shirt up, his intense gaze searing into mine. "What's going on is Ella May owes me a kiss on the chest."

"Yeah, she told us about that." Renee rounds the pool table and walks toward us. "I didn't realize she was going to do it now. Not that I have a problem with that." She seems pretty damn pleased as she ogles Micha.

Any amount of like I may have had for Renee, which wasn't a lot already, goes *poof*.

Micha's gaze remains fixed on me as he tugs his shirt over his head and drops it onto the floor.

While my eyes want to stray across his chest, I refuse to give him the satisfaction. Plus, there's no way in hell I'm going to openly check him out with everyone watching me. Instead, I let out a yawn and recline back against the sofa.

He chuckles, his eyes crinkling around the corners. "You can pretend to be bored all you want, but you're still going to have to pay up." His smug smirk is taunting me just enough that a spark of fire ignites inside me and wipes away any amount of nervousness I was feeling.

Squaring my shoulders, I stand up and step toward him. "You don't scare me, Micha Scott." That might not be true, though. Sometimes he scares me because of how he makes me feel.

"I guess this isn't a big deal then, is it?" His eyes glint with a dare.

"Nope, not at all." I dig up all the courage I have, pucker up, and then lean forward.

"Wait!" Jane calls out, and I freeze.

She jumps up from the sofa and holds up her finger. "Don't move. I have an idea." Then she hurries out of the room and into the bathroom.

Ethan enters the room then which, let me tell you, makes this whole thing that much more awesome—insert sarcasm on my part.

He takes one look at me, standing in front of a shirtless Micha, and his brow arches. "What'd I miss?" he asks.

"Ella lost a challenge this morning," Renee answers for me, tearing her eyes off

Micha's chest and focusing on Ethan. "She has to kiss Micha's chest. And may I add, a very un-hairy, toned chest." She flashes Micha a flirty smile, but his attention is still glued to me.

"You look nervous," he remarks.

I roll my eyes. "I'm never nervous."

"Liar."

"Show off."

"Pretty girl."

I point a finger at him. "Don't call me that."

His smile grows. "Pretty—"

"Got it," Jane announces as she dashes back into the room, holding something in her hand.

"Got what?" I wonder, turning toward her.

She sticks what she's holding out toward me. A tube of lipstick. "It's so we can all have proof that your lips really do touch his chest. Plus, it'll be super sexy."

"I like that idea," Micha says with a grin.

"I never agreed to lipstick," I point out.

"Is someone scared?" Steve taunts.

I glare at him. "You're not part of this, so shut it."

He holds up his hands in front of him. "Sorry. My bad. I was just trying to help." But a smirk resides on his lips.

Fucking Steve.

I glare at him one final time before looking back at Jane, who's still holding the tube of lipstick in my direction. I could put up a bigger fight. After all, lipstick wasn't part of the deal. But I don't want to seem like a chicken either, so I snatch up the lipstick and pull off the cap.

Great. It's bright red and will probably clash with my hair. But I guess that doesn't matter. I'll look stupid no matter what shade it is.

Sucking in a quiet breath, I put on the lipstick. Micha watches me intently, his teeth sunk into his bottom lip. Why he's looking at me like that is beyond me, and part of me questions if I even want to know.

Once I'm done, I recap the lipstick and hand it back to Jane.

"That's a good look for you," Micha says, biting his lip harder.

"Don't make fun of me," I reply, fidgeting with a leather band on my wrist.

"Oh, I'm not," he assures me, his gaze zeroing in on my lips. "You look really sexy right now."

"Micha," I warn.

He gives me an innocent look. "What? I was just giving you a compliment."

Deep down, I know that. But compliments have always made me uncomfortable.

"Let's just get this over with," I say with an exasperated exhale. Then, before I can chicken out, I lean forward and press my lips against his chest.

His skin is so soft and warm, is the thought that crosses my mind. But it's instantly squashed when Micha touches my waist, brushing his fingers along the skin that's peeking out between the hem of my shirt and the top of my jeans.

As heat flares through my body, I hurriedly slant back, pulling myself together just enough to put on a neutral expression.

Micha's expression is unreadable, but his gaze is intense as he stares at me.

"Challenge complete," I manage to get out evenly.

His gaze remains fused on me for a slamming heartbeat of a second before he glances down at the bright red lipstick on his chest. Then a ghost of a smile appears on his lips, no smugness evident, just ...

Happiness?

Is he happy I kissed his chest?

But as he meets my gaze, his smugness surfaces and my panic dissipates as I feel everything between us go back to normal.

"Still think my chest is hairy and gross?" he questions with a smirk.

"Yep. In fact, I think I have one of your hairs stuck to my lips ..." I pretend to pluck a hair from my lip.

He just smiles like I'm the most amusing person ever then reaches down to pick up his shirt. Once he pulls it on, Renee lets out a disappointed sigh. Then she heads back to the dartboard.

"Anyone want to play?" she asks.

Micha volunteers, and then I return to finishing my breakfast, trying to pretend like I don't have red lipstick on my mouth.

About a half an hour later, Micha has

returned to my side. It feels like things have returned to normal between us, although I do catch him touching his chest a couple of times with a weird look on his face. But then I get a text and, just like that, I'm thrown back to reality.

The reality that fun is a fleeting thing in my life.

"I have to go home," I mutter as I read the message Dean just sent me.

Dean: Hey, I just got a call from Mom. She's freakin' out because some cops stopped by and were asking her questions about some missing guy. I was going to go myself, but you're much better with these kinds of things.

Great. I guess Mrs. Mapleton didn't find her husband.

"What's wrong?" Micha asks, worry creasing between his brows.

I put my phone away and rise to my feet. "Dean just texted me and said Mom called him and was freaking out." I keep my voice quiet so no one else will hear me.

"Why can't he go check on her?" Micha asks in an annoyed tone.

I shrug. "He thinks I'm better at dealing with her, which I guess I am."

"Only because everyone makes you be," he mutters. Then he sighs and starts to stand up. "I'll go borrow Ethan's keys and drive you home."

I hold up my hand, indicating for him to stay put. "Steve and Jane are heading into town, so I'll just get a ride from them."

He frowns. "I don't mind driving you."

"I know you don't, but you don't need to." I zip up my jacket. "Stay here and have fun."

He looks like that's the last thing he wants to do, and I know if I asked him to come hang out with me today, he totally would. And part of me wants to ask him to, to let him make me feel better. But I hate putting my problems on him, and I don't like relying on people either. Plus, I don't think I'm ready to tell him that my mom might be having an affair with our crazy next-door neighbor's husband.

"I'll see you later, okay?" I tell him as I start toward the door so I can catch up with Steve and Jane.

"Do you still want me to spend the

night?" he calls out as I hurry toward the doorway.

Boy, do I want him to, partly because I'll be able to sleep better. But I don't want him to feel obligated.

"You don't have to," I say as I put my fingerless gloves back on.

He holds my gaze steadily. "I know that, but I want to."

Smashing my lips together, I nod. "Okay, cool."

He smiles but worry remains in his eyes. He looks that way a lot. He's always worrying about me. It makes me feel bad and guilty.

Micha is such a happy person, except when he's worrying about me. Sometimes I wish he'd stop, but the selfish part of me is glad he doesn't.

Glad I can rely on him.

One day, though, I know I'm going to have to stop relying on him so much. It'll suck, for sure, but it'll be for the better.

He deserves better than the crap that is my life.

THE REAL REASON

Micha

I hate watching her go, and it takes all my willpower not to get up and chase after her. If I had my way, I'd be with her all the time, but she won't let that to happen.

Ella and her walls. I wish I could find a way to crumble them.

"You look tired as hell," Ethan remarks as he sits down on the sofa beside me.

"Gee, thanks," I reply dryly, getting a cigarette out of my pack.

He takes a drag off his cigarette. "Sorry, but I was just stating a fact."

"I know." I sink back into the sofa and light up. "And I probably look tired as hell because I am tired as hell."

He smirks. "Did Ella keep you up all night."

He's always cracking jokes like that, about Ella and I hooking up, even though we never have. A lot of people think we have, though, and I can't really blame them. We spend a lot of time together. Plus, we sleep over at each other's houses sometimes. Although, lately I've been kind of taking a break from that, mostly because sleeping next to her has started ... well, to turn me on. I wish I could stop thinking about her like that, because it's complicating our relationship. But Ella is ... well, she's hot as hell and feisty and funny when she isn't buried in her life problems.

"I didn't even stay over at Ella's house last night." I move the end of the cigarette toward my lips as I stare off into empty space. "I had to wake up early this morning to shovel the driveway for my mom. The fucking snow won't let up."

But my excuse for not getting enough sleep is a lie.

I actually spent half the night staring out at Ella's bedroom window while I penned some new lyrics. Lyrics that are about her. But that's something I'm going to keep to myself because, for one, Ethan would tease the hell out of me. And two, Ella would freak out if she found out I was writing lyrics about her.

She gets weird about anything that has to do with emotions and her, something I know because I know her better than anyone else. And she knows me better than anyone else.

Although, there are a few things she doesn't know about me, like the real reason I don't spend as much time in her bed anymore, and why I probably won't wash this lipstick off my chest for a least a couple of days.

My hand drifts to my chest as I replay what it felt like to have her lips touch my skin. I mean, it's not like I've never had a girl kiss me before—even Ella has kissed me. But those red lips ... Jesus, she's so damn gorgeous. It's something I've been noticing more lately.

"You look stressed out," Ethan says as he puts his cigarette out in an ashtray. "You want to go up to The Hitch and spin donuts? I just got some new chains, so we should be able to get out if we get stuck."

I nod, relieved to have a distraction from thoughts of Ella.

At least, that's what I tell myself. Deep down, though, I know I'll continue to worry about her.

I always do.

A VOW

Ella

My mom won't tell me much of anything about what the police said. Only that they stopped by, looking for our neighbor. She's so worked up that I don't ask her if she's having an affair. If I do, it might push her over the edge.

So, instead, I spend most of the day taking care of her until she falls asleep. Then I clean the house and put a couple of bills in the mail. I want to go to the grocery store, but by the time I'm done with everything else, it's late and cold outside, so I decide to wait until tomorrow and trudge up the stairs to go to bed.

I skip taking a shower, even though I feel gross, and put on my pajamas. I glance out the window before I climb into bed, mostly to look at Micha's house. His bedroom light isn't on, so he's probably not home. I could call him and see where he is, but I don't want to be needy. Plus, he'd probably stop whatever he was doing and rush over to me, and I don't want him to do that.

So, I move back to climb into bed, but something catches my attention.

Mrs. Mapleton is standing on her front porch, wearing a robe, her arms crossed, and her gaze is locked on my house.

While I feel bad for her, I'm also kind of weirded out. I mean, this is the woman who chased Micha and me around the neighborhood with a knife.

I need to keep an eye on her, I vow to myself.

Of course, I'm not sure how I'm going to do that with how many responsibilities I have already. But I guess I'll have to figure it out.

Moving away from the window, I turn off the lights and climb into bed, burying myself in blankets to keep warm.

I spend the next thirty minutes tossing and turning, thinking I'm not going to get any sleep, but then I hear it—the window squeaking open.

A smile touches my lips, but I hastily erase it.

He doesn't say anything, but I hear him kicking off his boots and then shuffling off clothes as he probably removes his jacket. Then the blankets are being lifted up as he climbs into bed with me. The second his foot touches mine, I let out a squeal.

"Holy crap, you're freezing," I say, flipping over to face him.

His face is just a shadow in the darkness. "You better warm me up then."

"You're supposed to warm me up."

"Well, today we're switching places."

"Fine." I pretend to grimace then scoot toward him, trying to ignore that I'm a bit nervous.

Why am I nervous?

Once he wraps his arms around me, though, I relax a bit.

I can hear his heart thudding in his chest as I rest my head against it.

"I thought you weren't going to show up," I admit.

"Of course I'd show up. I always will," he promises. "And I wanted to be here earlier, but Ethan and I took his truck up to The Hitch and got it stuck. It took us hours to get it out."

"Sounds like fun." And compared to how I spent my day, it does.

"It really wasn't." He grows quiet for a moment. "I missed you."

I want to say it back—I really do—because I did miss him. But the words won't leave my lips. Instead, I press myself closer to him, and he tightens his arms around me.

"Thank you for coming over," I tell him quietly.

He tucks my head underneath my chin. "You don't have to thank me, Ella May. I like being here with you."

I'm not sure if he's telling the truth. I mean, who wants to be here at my house?

Even I don't most of the time, for many different reasons.

And only minutes later, one of those reasons makes a grand appearance as my dad stumbles into the house, ranting and raving about something. With all the banging going on, I assume he's drunk, and I worry he might come up here and yell at me for not bailing him out of jail. But thankfully, he never does. Either he passes out on the sofa or leaves. Still, I find it hard to relax.

Micha traces a path up and down my spine with his fingertips. "Relax, I got you."

He really does, too. And in that moment, I'm grateful he does. But in the back of my mind, I'm afraid. Afraid of when he realizes he doesn't want to deal with all my problems anymore.

I need to start taking care of myself more, I make another silent vow to do just that. Then I drift off to sleep, cuddled up to my best friend, grasping on to him while I still can, knowing that when I wake up in the morning, all this comfort will disappear as I'm forced to deal with a whole new set of problems.

ABOUT THE AUTHOR

Jessica Sorensen is a *New York Times* and *USA Today* bestselling author who lives in the snowy mountains of Wyoming. When she's not writing, she spends her time reading and hanging out with her family.

ALSO BY JESSICA SORENSEN

Also by Jessica Sorensen

The Mysteries of Star Grove:

Heat

Untitled (coming soon)

Signed with a Kiss:

Accepting the Deal

Untitled (coming soon)

My Life with the Band:

Discovering Benton

Untitled (coming soon)

Honeyton Annabella Series:

The Illusion of Annabella

Untitled (coming soon)

Rebels & Misfits:

Confessions of a Kleptomaniac

Untitled (coming soon)

Enchanted Chaos Series:

Enchanted Chaos

Shimmering Chaos

Untitled (coming soon)

The Breathing Undead Series:

Breathing Lies

Shadowed Whisperers (coming soon)

My Cursed Superhero Life:

Cursed

Untitled (coming soon)

Capturing Magic:

Chasing Wishes

Chasing Magic

Untitled (coming soon)

Chasing the Harlyton Sisters Series:

Chasing Hadley

Falling for Hadley

Holding onto Hadley

Untitled (coming soon)

Tangled Realms:

Forever Violet

Forever Stardust

Untitled (coming soon)

Curse of the Vampire Queen:

Tempting Raven

Enchanting Raven

Alluring Raven

Untitled (coming soon)

Unraveling You Series:

Unraveling You

Raveling You

Awakening You

Inspiring You

Every Single Breath

Untitled (coming soon)

Unexpected Series:

The Unexpected Complications of Revenge

Untitled (coming soon)

Shadow Cove Series:

What Lies in the Darkness

What Lies in the Dark

Untitled (coming soon)

Mystic Willow Bay Series:

The Secret Life of a Witch

Broken Magic

Stolen Kisses

One Wild, Crazy, Zombie Night

Magical Whispers & the Undead

Untitled (coming soon)

Standalones:

The Forgotten Girl

The Heartbreaker Society:

The Opposite of Ordinary

The Heartbreaker Society Curse (coming soon)

Broken City Series:

Nameless

Forsaken

Oblivion

Forbidden (coming soon)

Guardian Academy Series:

Entranced

Entangled

Enchanted

Entice

The Forest of Shadow and Bones

Untitled (coming soon)

Sunnyvale Series:

The Year I Became Isabella Anders

The Year of Falling in Love

The Year of Second Chances

Untitled (coming soon)

The Coincidence Series:

The Coincidence of Callie and Kayden

The Redemption of Callie and Kayden

The Destiny of Violet and Luke

The Probability of Violet and Luke

The Certainty of Violet and Luke

The Resolution of Callie and Kayden

Seth & Greyson

The Evermore of Callie & Kayden

Untitled (coming soon)

The Secret Series:

The Prelude of Ella and Micha

The Secret of Ella and Micha

The Forever of Ella and Micha

The Temptation of Lila and Ethan

The Ever After of Ella and Micha

Lila and Ethan: Forever and Always

Untitled (coming soon)

Ella and Micha: Infinitely and Always

The Shattered Promises Series:

Shattered Promises

Fractured Souls

Unbroken

Broken Visions

Scattered Ashes

Breaking Nova Series:

Breaking Nova

Saving Quinton

Delilah: The Making of Red

Nova and Quinton: No Regrets

Tristan: Finding Hope

Wreck Me

Ruin Me

Untitled (coming soon)

The Fallen Star Series:

The Fallen Star

The Underworld

The Vision

The Promise

The Lost Soul

The Evanescence

The Darkness Falls Series:

Darkness Falls

Darkness Breaks

Darkness Fades

The Death Collectors Series (NA and YA):

Ember X and Ember

Cinder X and Cinder

Spark X and Spark

Unbeautiful Series:

Unbeautiful

Untamed

ELSEWHERE
AND OTHER STORIES

GABRIEL-ALBERT AURIER (1865-1892) was an ardent member of the Symbolist Movement prior to his premature death from typhus. He was a regular contributor to *Le Décadent* before launching his own periodical, *Le Moderniste illustré* in 1889. He also assisted in the founding of the *Mercure de France*, whose associated press published his collected *Oeuvres posthumes* in 1893. He is now best remembered as an art critic, especially as a vociferous advocate of the work of Vincent van Gogh and Paul Gauguin.

BRIAN STABLEFORD has been publishing fiction and non-fiction for fifty years. His fiction includes an eighteen-volume series of "tales of the biotech revolution" and a series of half a dozen metaphysical fantasies set in Paris in the 1840s, featuring Edgar Poe's Auguste Dupin. His most recent non-fiction projects are *New Atlantis: A Narrative History of British Scientific Romance* (Wildside Press, 2016) and *The Plurality of Imaginary Worlds: The Evolution of French* roman scientifique (Black Coat Press, 2016); in association with the latter he has translated approximately a hundred and fifty volumes of texts not previously available in English, similarly issued by Black Coat Press.